Lost Haven

Lost Haven

First Edition

Copyright © 2014 by Sabrina A. Fish

Published by Babylon Books

ISBN: 978-0692209745

William Bernhardt's

Lost Haven
(Shine 7)

Sabrina A. Fish

The Shine Stories

By William Bernhardt

Childhood's End (Shine 1)
Roses in the Ashes (Shine 2)
Pandora's Daughters (Shine 3)
Renegades (Shine 4)
Who's Gonna Stop Me? (Shine 5)

By Tamara Grantham

Raze (Shine 6)

By Sabrina A Fish

Lost Haven (Shine 7)

By Burke Holbrook

The Unfound (Shine 8)

By Lara Wells

Cassandra (Shine 9)

For my God, who gave me all the tools to make my dream a reality: a supportive family, a wild imagination, and a stubborn streak a mile wide.

Nothing in the world is worth having or worth doing unless it means effort, pain, difficulty... I have never in my life envied a human being who led an easy life. I have envied a great many people who led difficult lives and led them well.

Theodore Roosevelt

1

Camille gasped in jagged breaths as she pushed through the crowd of laughing people. An angry male voice yelled her name. She moved faster. Loud music, bright flashing lights, and the smell of sweat and garbage swirled around her. Carnies called for her to try her luck to win one of the giant stuffed prizes hanging above their game stalls, but she ignored them to search for the corridor of food carts. She rounded the corner, encountering smells of sweet fried funnel cakes, sizzling turkey legs, and grilled sweet corn on the cob. Her stomach churned, the smells failing to entice like they normally would.

She was supposed to meet her best friend, Jenni, at the sarsaparilla stand. Each September, they enjoyed coming to Oklahoma's State Fair. The first thing they always did was buy the little mini milk jug of iced root beer. Knowing the stand was usually located at the center of the main corridor of food vendors, Camille searched for the correct way to run. Unsure, but knowing she needed to keep moving, she lunged to the right only to have two large hairy arms wrap around her from behind.

Her ex-boyfriend, Gary, spun her around and brought his mouth down on hers before she could call out for help. Holding her against his heavily muscled chest, Gary pulled her into the shadows as a group of teenage males whistled and called for them to get a room. His large hand held her head still while his other arm pinned her arms to her sides. She kicked at his shins, but he forced his tongue into her mouth. Realizing she would tire long before he would, she went limp.

1

He groaned in triumph. Ignoring the bile threatening to come up, she bit down on his tongue as hard as she could while bringing her knee up into his crotch. He jerked his head back, releasing her as he cried out and crumpled to the ground.

She glared at him. "It's over, Gary. Touch me again, and I'll file a VPO against your ass."

She backed out of the shadows into the crowded, brightly lit avenue between the food carts. He straightened to his full six-feet-one-inch height and smiled at her. The cold possessiveness in his pale blue eyes raked over her body. She shivered. Had she ever found that possessiveness attractive?

They'd dated for a year until her parents' deaths six months ago. With her parents no longer in the picture, he'd stopped pretending to be the kind, considerate man she'd been attracted to. He'd begun to use her grief against her, undermining her confidence in herself until she'd believed she was nothing without him. Then he'd put his hands on her. She'd actually believed him when he'd said it was her fault. If Jenni hadn't stepped in, she'd have married and given him total control of her life. She shuddered. She'd been so naïve.

Gary followed her into the lighted corridor. "No one will believe you. You belong to me, Camille. There's no where you can go. If you try to run, I'll find you."

She squeezed her shaking hands into fists. Her breath rushed in and out of her lungs as the truth of his words threatened to choke her. Pressure tightened in her chest. She stepped back as he moved closer. People gave them wary glances, sensing the thick tension between them.

"No. I belong only to myself. We're done. Leave me alone."

"Why do you fight the inevitable? You know I'll care

for you better than you ever could. You'll have everything you could ever want." He held his hand out to her. "Come, Camille. Stop being ridiculous. Let me take you home, where you belong."

Her parents hadn't been happy when they'd first started dating. Her father had been sure that ulterior motives were involved. But after a year of his perfect courting of their daughter, even her father changed his mind. Her parents had been so happy when they'd announced that they'd be getting married. They'd thought Gary made her happy. He'd been everything they'd wanted in a son-in-law.

Yes, he hit her once, but hadn't she brought it on herself? Hadn't she pushed him to it with her accusations? She'd found the papers demanding her father sell their land to Gary's grandfather. Suddenly Gary's mindless pursuit of her had seemed like a means to an end. She'd been sure he didn't want her for herself, but for the land his family coveted. She'd thrown the papers in his face. She'd screamed that he was nothing but a whore selling his body for her family's land. And he'd backhanded her so hard the entire right side of her face became a large, ugly bruise.

She looked at his outstretched hand, then up to his cold blue gaze. She remembered the pain of his hand. The cruelty in his face when she'd accused him of whoring himself.

He hadn't denied it.

Straightening her shoulders, she backed away. His eyebrows lowered. A hand touched her shoulder, offering support. Camille met Jenni's steady gaze. Her friend squeezed her shoulder. Camille stepped back, taking Jenni's hand in hers.

She lifted her chin and met Gary's icy glare. "It's over. I will never let you back into my life. Your threats are nothing but the hot air of a pathetic man who can't accept rejection."

She pulled Jenni until they stood on the opposite side of the wide corridor of food carts. His brows lowered further as something dangerous moved through his eyes.

The hairs on her arms stood up.

Her head pulsed at the base of her skull. Clenching Jenni's hand, she pulled her friend backwards to get further away from him. "I wish I'd never met you, Gary Walker. I wish you couldn't see me, that you were blind. I wish your cold blue eyes could never again touch me with their cruelty. I hate you."

His face darkened as his chest heaved with his anger. His eyes stayed focused on her.

Jenni pulled on her arm. "Come on, Camille. He can't do anything to us. Let's go enjoy the fair."

When Jenni pulled her away, Gary exploded toward them. The crowd between them cleared as people stumbled out of the way.

Camille froze.

But before Gary could take more than a step, he cried out, collapsed to his knees and clutched at his head.

Jenni pulled Camille's arm, but she couldn't move. He seemed to be in real pain.

A man standing near Gary knelt down and put his hand on Gary's back. "Sir, do you need help?"

Gary groaned and squinted at the man. His eyes widened and he grabbed the other man's arm. "My head. It feels like someone took a pickaxe to it. I can't see anything."

The man pulled out a cell phone and dialed. "Yes, this is Dr. Marsh. I need an ambulance for a possible aneurism at the fairgrounds."

Gary turned his unfocused gaze toward her. "She did this to me."

LOST HAVEN

The air left Camille's chest in a rush. Clenching her friend's arm, she struggled to force air into her lungs.

He was right. She had done it.

She'd blinded Gary with her Shine.

2

Camille tapped her tablet and Sentinel's news site appeared. She scanned the headlines, smiling at the picture of Mrs. Jenkin's one-hundredth birthday celebration.

Her smile faded as she read the next headline. The SSS were hosting their weekly luncheon tomorrow at the Baptist church. Nearly the entire town could be found on the member list thanks to Gary and his new cause. Small-minded bigots. They hated out of fear and ignorance. She slid her finger across the tablet.

The classifieds appeared. She caught her breath. Highlighted at the top of the screen, the words LAND FOR SALE glared at her.

The tablet vibrated.

A picture of Dr. O'Brien, her employer and Sentinel's lone optometrist, replaced the newspaper. She touched the picture and forced a smile as the doctor himself appeared on the video chat screen. "Good morning, Doctor."

"Good morning, Camille," he said, his voice thick with congestion. "I'm afraid I've come down with something. Reschedule my appointments and close the office for the day when you leave for lunch."

The lines on the older man's face appeared deeper around tired eyes and his usually neat white hair stuck out in a disheveled mess.

She suppressed a sigh of relief. "Don't worry about the office. I'll take care of everything. You get better."

The doctor nodded and the video chat window closed, revealing the news site once again. Forcing herself to ignore the ad she'd paid for earlier that morning, she pulled up the appointment list for the day and began calling the patients to reschedule. She finished the last call and closed the appointment screen, glancing around the office and cozy waiting room, her home away from home. The familiar fragrance of homemade vanilla and clove potpourri failed to calm her. On the tablet, her reflection was superimposed over the ad she didn't want to see. She glared at her ordinary long brown hair with light brown eyes located in a fair, round face. If only she was as average as her appearance suggested.

Pushing her useless wishes from her mind, she focused on the news site. The news staff hadn't wasted any time posting her ad. She scanned the item responsible for ruining her day.

LAND FOR SALE

300 acres 10 miles south of Sentinel

1,500 sq. ft log home on north end of property, 2-story, 3 bedroom, 2.5 bath, renovated in last 5 years, 2 car garage. 11 acre pond, surrounded by trees.

Contact: Camille Leon at 555-4657

She clenched her jaw. Every part of her wanted to call and demand the ad be taken down. She didn't want to sell the land her family had owned since Oklahoma's land-run days, but she had no choice. As the only technician to a small-town optometrist, her salary wasn't big enough to cover the mountain of debt left by her parents' sudden deaths. Her father had been terrible with money. It didn't help that her parents' deaths hadn't been covered under the terms of her father's life insurance policy either. She'd tried telling them that her father wouldn't have killed himself much less her mother, but the smug insurance agent hadn't believed her. Her father loved her mother. They'd just celebrated their twenty-fifth anniversary the day before their deaths six months ago.

She closed her eyes, refusing to let tears fall. Her father didn't kill her mother or himself. She knew it. And she suspected she knew who was responsible. Mr. Walker had been pressuring her father to sell their land for years, even going so far as to have his grandson, Gary, court and almost marry Camille. Guilt weighed down her shoulders. Now, thanks to an aneurism, Gary was forever considered legally blind. Oh, he could see with the help of glasses, just not well. Jenni tried to convince her that his loss of eyesight wasn't her fault, but Camille wasn't sure. Her Shine affected the sight. Even if an aneurism had existed behind his eyes, could her power have been the reason it exploded at the fair?

She pushed her guilt over Gary from her mind. Camille resisted the urge to throw the tablet across the room and instead hit the power button. Her parents had been gone six months and though she'd done everything she could to keep from selling, her savings were almost depleted. She had to sell, but it wouldn't be to the Walkers. She'd take half of what the land was worth before she'd sell to those murderers.

3

The old-style bell rang. Camille left the charts she'd been filing with a sigh, resisting the urge to Shine. She'd refused to use her gift since the incident at the fair. The one day she craved solitude would be the day the bell rang over and over. She glanced at the clock. Almost lunch time.

She pasted a smile on her face as she rounded the corner into the reception room. A short, black headed woman opened her arms. Her emotions surged to the surface as she stepped into her best friend's embrace.

"I saw the ad and knew you'd be taking it hard," Jenni said.

"I want to call and demand they remove it, but I can't." She squeezed her friend in a tight hug, and then stepped back. "What will I do without my sanctuary?"

"You'll make another one." The Asian woman's exotic eyes twinkled as she pulled a piece of paper out of her purse. "I've got a list of cute little properties for sale in town, several with extensive gardens that should give you that privacy you want."

"House hunting?" Her stomach turned. "Sounds like a complete happy meal."

Jenni grabbed her hand. "Take this. Think about it. We can pretend we're on one of those shows on T.V. It'll be fun, I promise."

She smiled despite herself. Jenni's serene presence always made her feel better in any situation. She'd never seen her friend struggle to contain her emotions. "I'll look at it later."

Jenni lifted an eyebrow.

"Promise. Don't you have a yoga lesson or a meditation class to get to?"

Jenni nodded. "Yes, I have a session at the retirement center and yoga with the bridge club ladies after that. Wanna meet at Smokey's for drinks and dancing tonight? My treat."

She nodded. Being alone with her thoughts would be worse, especially without any work to distract her. "Order me a drink if you get there first."

Jenni winked and left. She returned to her charts. The bell rang again.

"I'm going to look at the li--" Her voice froze.

Mr. Walker met her gaze, his gray eyebrows rising over cold blue eyes. Every muscle locked in place as the urge to throw the file at him washed through her.

He towered over her. His shiny, black cowboy boots clicked on the hard wood floor, and reminded her of a scene in a horror movie. She curled her fingers to keep from jumping on him and clawing his eyes out. She knew he had something to do with her parents' deaths even if nobody believed her.

Her heart pounded in her ears. "Get out."

"Come now, Miss Leon. This was a public office last I checked." He purred in a soft Southern drawl.

She pivoted, returning to the shelf where she'd been working. She paused before rounding the corner. "Dr. O'Brien is sick today, though you're welcome to make an appointment and come back another time." Her voice hardened. "Then you can leave."

"But I'm interested in your land. It is for sale, is it not?"

She picked up a chart from the stack and fought the urge to Shine. "You weren't invited to this rodeo, Mr. Walker."

"Your ad didn't say it was by invitation only. I'm prepared to pay top dollar."

"I'm not interested in your tainted money."

He stepped closer, lowering his voice. "Who do you think has been keeping my grandson from sic'ing his SSS zealots on you?" Camille's eyes widened as she met the old man's hard gaze. "I can make your life very difficult."

She clenched her jaw. "I'll donate the land to charity before I'll sell to you."

"We'll see, Miss Leon. We'll see."

He turned and left her standing in a cold sweat, her emotions swirling inside her. The beeping of her tablet pulled her out of it. Taking a deep breath, she sank into her chair and slid her shaking finger across the screen. A good-looking blond man, about ten years her senior, appeared on the screen.

She pasted a smile on her face. "Good morning, Dr. O'Brien's office. How can I help you?"

The man returned her smile with an equally fake one of his own. "My name is John Marks. I'm an attorney out of Weatherford. I have a client interested in the three-hundred acres for sale south of Sentinel. Are you Camille Leon?"

Her knuckles turned white as she gripped the tablet.

The attorney's eyebrows inched up his forehead. "Am I speaking with Camille Leon?"

"Yes, I'm Camille."

"Good. My client is very interested in your property and would like to meet with you. He has the late afternoon and evening free today or the morning free tomorrow."

Today? Her fingers pleated the purple fabric of her favorite scrub top. "I can meet him in the Sentinel Diner at five."

The attorney nodded. "Very good. We'll see you then, Ms. Leon."

Ignoring the sick flop of her stomach, she grabbed her tablet and Jenni's list, and locked up the office. She hoped the attorney's client was serious. She'd sell it to them at half the price just to keep it out of Mr. Walker's hands.

4

Camille stared across the table at John Marks and his client, Gregg Jeffries. Mr. Jeffries described plans to put a private rehabilitation facility on her land. They each wore suits, neatly pressed, with conservative ties. She was certain an entire can of hair spray had gone into keeping their thick hair in place and she was sure that Mr. Jeffries wore concealer under his eyes. Did he do cucumber treatments at night, as well? Probably.

The attorney placed the contract on the table. "Our terms are listed here. We're prepared to offer top dollar, Ms. Leon. I think you'll find we're more than fair and much higher than any other offer you're likely to receive."

The contract, a magnet drawing her gaze, made it difficult to pay attention to the conversation. Was she really doing this? A headache pulsed in her right temple.

"We believe the price we're offering and our plans for the property will sway you in our direction. Our goal is to help young women get their lives back."

She shifted in her seat as her stomach clenched. "What kind of rehab will this be, Mr. Jeffries?"

"We take young women who've been born into an unfortunate circumstance, who are unable to fit into society, and we work to give them a second chance," Jeffries replied.

She forced a smile as her heart sank. "That sounds like an admirable facility, Mr. Jeffries." She shuffled the pages of the contract together and put them to the side. "I have several offers already, and I want to look at each contract and consider what each of you will be doing with the land before I make my decision. I'll give you a call by the end of the week."

After shaking their hands and walking them out of the diner, she returned to the booth and turned on her tablet. She pulled up a search engine and typed in Jeffries' name.

Just as she'd suspected. The window filled with a list of articles involving one of the Shine rehab facilities in West Texas where he'd made a name for himself as an assistant director. She laid her head on the desk. Allowing one of the Shine rehab facilities to be built on her land was not an option.

Shine abilities appeared publicly seven years ago, though Camille gained her abilities long before that. It was said to be a genetic phenomenon that affected only girls, special abilities having mostly to do with the brain and manipulating it. Non-Shines feared these special abilities. She figured they were just jealous.

The Shine Surveillance Society was a group of fanatics focused on harassing any woman possessing Shine abilities. They blamed every natural disaster or terrorist attack on Shine. Just after her parents' deaths six months ago, an explosion, blamed on a Shine, had taken out the entire city of Seattle, killing hundreds. Then two months ago, another explosion leveled Santa Monica. The Shine was killed in that one.

The government was already working on legislation to deal with Shines. As it was, any Shine discovered was sent to one of the government's rehabilitation facilities for evaluation. Once you went into one, you never came out.

So much for selling her land this week and keeping it out of Mr. Walker's hands. She sighed. Nothing was ever easy.

5

Camille scanned the busy pub as someone butchered an old version of *I Love Rock & Roll*. She shouldn't have agreed to this tonight. She didn't feel like laughing and though she usually loved karaoke, she wasn't feeling much like singing or dancing either. A mountain of their favorite chicken nachos sat in front of her along with her drink of choice, vodka and cranberry juice.

She squeezed the lime wedge into the drink. "I needed this."

"Meeting not go well?" Jenni asked, as she sipped on a glass of chardonnay the pub's owner ordered in just for her.

She shook her head and focused on the drunk girl up on the stage. She wasn't going to tear up and look like a mushy dog biscuit the rest of the night. She gulped her drink and grimaced as the vodka burned down her throat. A double shot. Nice. Jenni knew her so well.

She sipped the next drink and picked at the nachos. "Greg Jeffries is the assistant director for the Shine Rehabilitation Center in West Texas. He wants to build a new rehab facility on my land." Jenni's face paled as Camille continued. "He's convinced that his worthy use of the land and his hefty offer will convince me to sell to him."

"Will it?"

"When pigs fly."

"But what will you do now? You have no other offers."

"Mr. Walker came by the office today," Camille muttered.

Jenni's eyes widened. "And you didn't do him bodily harm?"

15

"I wanted to, but common sense prevailed. This time."

Jenni squeezed her hand. "It'll all work out, Cam. God has a way of seeing that His children are taken care of. Pray about it. You'll see."

She nodded, but even knowing her friend was right, she still couldn't get rid of the knot in her stomach.

Jenni glanced toward the bar. A smile spread across her face and she waved at a tall man sitting by himself. Michael Saunders, the sheriff's son. He'd been three years their senior and they both had schoolgirl crushes on him and his bright blue eyes, thick brown hair, and tall lean athlete's body. He'd been away at college and she hadn't realized he was back in town.

"Why are you waving like a lunatic at Michael Saunders?"

Jenni rolled her eyes. "He just graduated from OSU's veterinary school. He works at my dad's clinic."

She heard a note of interest in her friend's voice and Jenni's olive cheeks were definitely reddening. "Oh my Gandhi. You like him."

"Hush, he's coming over." Jenni smiled as the man stepped up to their table. "Hi Michael. You remember Camille Leon, don't you?"

His handsome blue eyes glanced her way. "Hey Camille, good to see you again." His gaze shifted back to Jenni.

She knew when she was in the way. "I need to get home. It's been a long day. I'll catch up with you guys later."

6

Camille sighed as she turned off the highway onto her property. She followed the long drive around her home to the garage that made up the bottom level of a large log cabin built into the side of a hill. The cabin was much too big for her and took hours to clean, but she still didn't want to sell it. She'd hoped to one day raise a family of her own here. Her parents always intended to fill it with children, but hadn't been able to conceive after Camille. They'd considered alternative methods, but Camille's Shine ability changed everything. They hadn't said, but she knew they'd worried about having another child that might develop the Shine gene. She could still remember the look on their faces that first time.

She'd been sitting at the breakfast table, upset because she couldn't find her school shirt for School Spirit Day. All of her friends would be wearing theirs and she'd be mortified to stand out by not having hers.

Her mother had hugged her. "It's only a shirt, baby. I'll look for it while you're at school and you'll have it for the next spirit day."

"But Mom, I'll stand out. They'll make fun of me," she'd wailed, terrified that standing out would make her the center of the other kids' ridicule. "I wish I could disappear."

Her mother had smiled down at her and wiped the tears from her face. She closed her eyes, imagining herself fading from her mother's sight. The back of her head pulsed as tiny lines flashed behind her eyelids. Without thinking, she'd reached out and rearranged the tiny pattern of lights, her mind filling with relief. She'd opened her eyes to see her mother still reaching toward her, as if only half a second had passed. Then her mother's face had paled. She'd squeezed Camille's arm under one hand while patting her face under the other. "Cam? Camille? Say something to me, honey."

Her father had come running. "What's wrong?"

"Mom?" She looked down at herself, alarmed at the fear in their faces.

Her mother spoke. "She's here. I can feel her and I can hear her, but I can't see her. Can you see her?"

She yelled, trying to make the pulsing at the back of her head stop. "Mom, I'm right here. See? I'm right here."

Her mother pulled Camille into her arms. "Thank God."

"Ron, tell me you saw that," her mother asked, voice shaking.

He stared at his daughter. "Cam, can you do that again?"

"Do what, Daddy?"

"You were invisible, baby. We could hear you," he glanced at her mother, "and we could feel you, but we couldn't see you."

A rushing sound filled her ears. "I was right here the whole time, Daddy. I didn't disappear."

"Right before you vanished, you said you wanted to disappear. Do you remember what you were thinking? How you felt?"

She reached a hand to touch the back of her head. "Mommy, what's wrong with me?"

Her mother pulled her in close. "It's okay, baby. Maybe you should stay home today. You won't have to worry about not having your shirt and I can make sure it doesn't happen again over the weekend."

Her entire life changed that day. Every time she imagined being some sort of sideshow freak, the lines appeared behind her eyes and she vanished from sight. Her parents pulled her from public school and homeschooled her.

They became obsessed with learning about the brain and how it worked. The first time she'd seen an image of the eye and the many tiny nerves in it, she'd known that was what she saw when she Shined. She'd learned that it was her occipital lobe that pulsed. With this knowledge she'd learned to control her ability, though she never forgot the look of fear in her parents' eyes that first time. Had they been afraid of her or for her? They never said, though they did everything to protect her.

She'd give anything to have them back. Loving her and loving each other.

She entered her home and flipped the kitchen light switch. She froze. Her possessions lay strewn across the floor, furniture upturned, drawers pulled open. Tears filled her eyes at the sight of shattered pictures frames and photos crumpled on the floor.

She heard something upstairs. *Shine, Camille!*

She closed her eyes and saw two groups of tiny lines on the backs of her eyelids. A pulsing began at the back of her head. The lines formed the loose shape of two human eyes and each group led to a larger thicker line that she now knew was the optic nerve. She followed tiny specs of pulsing light through each optic nerve until they intersected at the optic chiasm, then she stopped the tiny patterns of light. Manipulating the patterns, she pictured the house without her in it. She sent the command out like a radio tower broadcasting a signal. It took only a second.

She double-tapped the emergency icon on her tablet, then tiptoed to the stairs. Hearing nothing, she eased up the stairs, straining to see into the darkened hallway. A beam of light flashed inside her parents' room. She caught her breath. That door, always tightly sealed, kept the last traces of her parents' scents from fading. Her heart pounded as she slid her feet across the carpet, avoiding the weak places in the hallway, until she could see inside.

A shadow moved to the door. "Gandhi's teeth, she's in the house." The shadow turned back into the room. "We have to go. Now."

"We haven't found it yet," a female voice muttered.

"She'll have noticed the mess by now. We have to go."

The female's shadow joined the other. "That file is here somewhere. The Reverend won't be happy if we don't find it."

Flashing lights lit the windows at the front of the house. "We can't try again if we're sitting in jail. Let's go."

The two shadows disappeared into her parents' room, reappearing in front of the balcony doors. Camille stepped into the room as they opened the door. Her foot collided with something hard on the floor. The intruders swung their flashlight beams across the room, passing over her.

"Someone's in here."

"You'd have seen her if she'd come up the stairs. Stop being a nervous ninny and let's go."

The first shadow slipped out the patio doors.

Camille reached for the object she'd kicked, her father's shoe, and hurled it at the second intruder. It hit him in the back of the head and he lurched out the door.

"What the--" he looked back over his shoulder.

The other shadow pulled him up. "You're a damned klutz, Drew. Let's get out of here."

The male intruder yanked his arm from his partner's grasp and looked back toward the room, his narrow gaze lit by moonlight. Camille memorized the square jaw, broken nose, and military haircut. She'd know that face if she ever saw it again. She stepped up to the railing to watch them disappear into the trees behind her home.

Someone, most likely the Sheriff, banged on her front door. She stilled her Shine as she ran down the stairs to let him in. The intruders hadn't found what they were looking for. Determination made her straighten her shoulders. She'd find it before they returned.

7

Camille dragged a finger through the dust that lay over every surface of her home. All the technology in the world and the police still used this antiquated method of gathering fingerprints.

Yawning, she rubbed her forehead while reaching for the broom. She'd been up all night, but she didn't bother lying down. She wouldn't be able to sleep while her home looked like this. Sighing, she swept the dust, papers, and glass into a pile in the center of the living room's hard wood floors then pushed furniture back into place.

When the great room and kitchen looked as they should, she went into her father's personal library and surveyed the torn books and overturned furniture. Her father had loved collecting rare books and had been responsible for her love for them as well. She reached for her father's favorite, *To Kill a Mockingbird*, and tenderly swept the dust from its cover. He'd often compared the treatment of Shines to that of Tom Robinson, guilty until proven innocent. Had he lived to see the outcome of the Seattle tragedy, he'd have given her his "I told you so" look.

She thanked God that her parents hadn't taken her to a doctor when her Shine appeared. Lack of documentation kept her safe from those like the SSS who targeted Shines, and the authorities who detained Shines.

She heaved the overturned desk and picked up the large three-tiered trophy her father and mother won as a team in an adult bowling league. It had held the place of honor on the mantle of the office fireplace, the only trophy her father ever won. Now it lay crushed, the rods holding it together wrenched from the wooden base.

LOST HAVEN

She gently gathered the pieces of the trophy into her arms. She held her breath, afraid to drop anything and damage the trophy further. She grabbed two sizes of nut drivers, a handful of washers, extra nuts, and a hammer then returned to the kitchen. She wouldn't allow the intruders to win by leaving the trophy a broken mess.

She used the driver to remove the nuts and pulled the rods from the base. She pressed the MDF wood into place around the holes and twisted a nut onto the first rod, followed by a washer. She threaded that rod back through its hole and put a second washer and nut on, leaving it loose until she could do the same with the other two. Reaching for the second rod, she straightened the shiny gold columns around the rods.

She reached her fingers into the second column for its rod and her fingers slipped over a cold, plastic lump. She pulled the column toward her and looked inside. Fingers shaking, she reached inside and pulled out a small, black thumb drive.

8

The thumb drive burned a hole in Camille's pocket as she knocked on Jenni's door. Dr. Pham, her friend's father, opened the door and waved her in.

"Camille," he said, a concerned frown on his face. "Jenni told me about the break-in. I'm glad you weren't harmed."

"Thank you for allowing me to stay here tonight, Dr. Pham."

He waved away her thanks. "You're like a daughter to me and you're welcome any time."

Jenni appeared at the top of the stairs. She smiled at Dr. Pham as he bowed and disappeared into the house. She followed Jenni to her room. Her heart pounded as she slipped her hand into her pocket and closed it around the thumb drive

Jenni threw her arms around her. "I'm glad you're alright. I can't believe you walked in on the intruders. You could have been hurt or worse."

She held the thumb drive up. "I know what they're after."

She told Jenni about sneaking upstairs and overhearing the intruders talking about a file.

Jenni's eyes narrowed. "Maybe we should just destroy it."

"What if there's proof that my dad is innocent?"

Jenni eyed the thumb drive warily. "All right. But it feels like a bad idea."

Camille pulled out her tablet and stuck the thumb drive into the port. She tapped to open the file that appeared on the screen. A security box appeared.

"Razor. It needs a password."

"Well, what password would your father have used?"

Her thoughts raced in circles. Her father had been an architect working for A New Beginning Church, a mega church with its main base in Oklahoma City. Her father's office had been located at the Clinton branch located about twenty-five minutes northeast of Sentinel. He'd been one of a team of architects responsible for the current design used for the new branches being built around the United States. His area of expertise had been the kids' section of the church. He'd been proud that his work had been enjoyed by children from all over.

Also the Clinton branch's resident computer tech, he'd been responsible for handling the minor issues the branch might have and contacting the IT department at the main office in Oklahoma City when bigger issues arose.

He'd been terrible at handling money, believing that you couldn't take it with you when you died and so you might as well use it to help others. It had been the only subject over which he and her mother had argued and was the reason she now had to sell.

She typed in her name.

WRONG PASSWORD

She typed her mother's name.

WRONG PASSWORD

She tried a half dozen others, with no success. She slammed her hand against the tablet. "I have no idea what it could be."

Jenni heaved a relieved sigh. "Maybe it's better this way. If you don't know what information is on it, the people who want it will leave you alone."

"My father left it for me to find." She tossed it on the bed. "I need a safe place to hide it until I can figure out the password."

Jenni picked it up and sat on the bed beside her. "It's too bad you can't use your Shine to hide anything or anyone but yourself. Then it'd be safe anywhere."

She'd never actually tried to hide anything other than herself. Picturing Jenni's room and the two of them sitting in it, she focused on the thumb drive and Shined.

"Razor." Her friend's breathless voice broke the silence.

Heart pounding, she focused on her friend.

Jenni glanced up at her, eyes wide. "I can still feel it there, but I can't see it." She looked back down at her hand. "There's not even a shadow to give it away."

Camille peered closer. "I can only affect what those in range of my power see or perceive with their eyes. Someone can still feel and hear me. It appears it's the same with inanimate objects."

A thoughtful look crossed Jenni's face as she laid the thumb drive on the bed. "If you can do this, how much more can you do?"

Camille scowled. "No. What if I try to use my power on you and I hurt you like I did Gary?"

Jenni rolled her eyes. "You didn't hurt the big idiot. That aneurism was just waiting for the right stress to push it over the edge. All you did was not listen to his lies. Don't let him chainmail you again, Cam."

She wiped her damp palms on the legs of her jeans. "I couldn't live with myself if I hurt you too."

Jenni placed her hands on Camille's shoulders. "You've used your power on me and others many times since it manifested. Was anyone else ever hurt? Ever?"

Her friend was right. She wouldn't let Gary's poison taint her use of this gift she'd been given.

She smiled. "Want to see if you can walk by your father without him seeing you?"

Jenni laughed. "Rock and Razor."

9

Camille stared into her glass while Jenni and Michael made goo-goo eyes with each other on the dance floor. The song, slow, romantic, and exactly opposite of her mood, made her want to stuff cotton in her ears. The thumb drive hung from a chain around her neck. No matter how hard she tried, she couldn't think of the password.

Camille's excitement at being able to make her, Jenni, and the thumb drive disappear had soon dimmed as she'd returned to trying to think of the thumb drive's password earlier that day. Jenni, tired of an afternoon wasted thinking up every possible password to do with Camille's father, insisted they needed to clear their heads and go out.

So here they were, again, at Smokey's Pub. Michael had been waiting, of course. Camille rolled her eyes and finished her drink before standing and pushing through the crowd toward the ladies room. Upon seeing the long line, she abruptly switched directions and collided with a hard, wide chest.

"Whoa there, careful," a husky voice rumbled from deep in the chest under the palms of her hands.

Her face warming, Camille looked up and met twinkling pale blue eyes set in the most handsome face she'd ever seen. "Sorry. I saw the long line for the ladies room and decided I didn't need to go that bad," she babbled, her face getting hotter.

He smiled and leaned closer, his shaggy blond curls sweeping into his eyes. "Sorry, but I think you owe me a drink."

Camille tore her gaze from his and looked dumbly at his hands and then the floor. "What do you mean?"

He pulled her chin up so that she was forced to meet his mesmerizing gaze again. "Well, if I'd had one, you would have spilled it on me and I would have had a reason to enjoy your company longer. So now I'm just going to pretend I did and correct that oversight."

Camille smiled. "Is that right?"

He widened his eyes and nodded his head in his best little boy interpretation. "Yes, ma'am."

Camille laughed at his exaggerated southern accent, charmed by his old world manners as he swept his arm toward the bar and held out his elbow to escort her. "So tell me, pretty lady, what brings you to Smokey's Pub, other than God's plan that we meet?"

She shook her head and climbed on the bar stool he indicated, blushing under the focus of his attention. "I'm here with friends." She turned toward the dance floor and pointed to Jenni and Michael.

"From the way Saunders is looking at your girlfriend, I'd say you're a bit of a third wheel, which works out just perfect for me," he said, a roguish grin on his face.

Camille thought she'd never blushed so much in her life as she lowered her gaze. He made her feel awkward and tongue tied, as if she were still in high school.

Camille held out her hand. "I'm Camille Leon."

His smile slipped and he rubbed a hand over the back of his neck. She lifted an eyebrow and his smile returned as he took hold of her hand, turned it, and kissed her knuckles. He held her gaze and heat spread through her body with the press of his warm lips. "It's nice to meet you, Camille. I'm Jeremy."

Camille started to ask what was wrong, but Jeremy pulled her onto the dance floor. The feel of his hard body

29

pressed against hers scattered her thoughts. The slow song no longer grated on her nerves, but made her think of his lips. Would they feel as soft as they had on her knuckles? Camille couldn't believe she was thinking this way about someone she'd just met. His mouth lifted in a smile and she realized she was staring and he knew it. Her gaze jumped up to meet laughing blue eyes. His smile melted. His eyes dropped and she darted out her tongue to wet her lips.

He leaned toward her and she froze, unable to pull away.

A cool hand touched her shoulder and she jumped, the trance he cast over her broken. Jenni and Michael stood next to them, curiosity in both their gazes. "Would you like to bring your new friend over to sit with us, Cam?"

Camille flushed again and her friend's eyes widened. "Jeremy, this is Jenni Pham and you know Michael Saunders."

Michael held his hand out. "It's been a long time, Walker."

Jeremy flinched and glanced toward Camille as she stiffened and her jaw dropped. "Walker? Jeremy Walker? As in George Walker's grandson? Gary Walker's absent older brother?" Camille pulled away, berating herself for being seven kinds of fool. "You're good Mr. Walker. You almost had me." She met his narrowed eyes with an icy glare. "No, Jenni, I don't think my new 'friend' will be sitting with us."

He grabbed her arm. "Wait, Camille, it isn't like that." She glared down at his hand on her arm, until he dropped it. "I didn't know who you were until you told me your name."

She raised an eyebrow. "And you didn't think to be honest and tell me when the opportunity presented itself?"

Jeremy glanced over at Michael and Jenni, who watched with open curiosity then back to Camille. "I know there's bad blood between you and my brother as well as you and the old man. Hell, there's bad blood between most people and the old man. I was enjoying being with you and didn't want to ruin it."

Camille gave Jenni a tight smile. "I have to go. I'll just walk to your place for my car and head home."

Jenni frowned. "But what about last night's intruders? Are you sure you should be out there alone?"

Jeremy's eyebrows lowered. "You had intruders? I'll take you home."

"I don't need any help from the likes of you, Mr. Walker," Camille growled before turning on her heel and walking out of the pub.

The humid summer heat hit her in the face, making her grimace. Five people paced on the sidewalk in front of the pub, large signs in their hands as they yelled at anyone nearby. *Alcohol leads to fornication which leads straight to hell. Repent of your sin. Don't follow Shines to hell. Dancing is devil worship. Shines use alcohol to take you to hell with them. Repent.*

Camille rolled her eyes and turned toward Jenni's house. This was a different group than had been here when she entered the bar. There must have been a shift change.

Their voices faded as she practically ran from the pub. How could she have not recognized those icy blue eyes so much like the Walker patriarch's? She was a fool. Her eyes burned with tears she refused to let fall.

The rumble of a truck pulled up alongside her and the passenger window lowered. "Get in, Camille."

She kept walking, refusing to acknowledge him in any way. He sighed and slowed to pull the truck over behind her so that she was highlighted by the headlights.

Gravel crunched under his shoes as he jogged up beside her. "You can't blame me for how my grandfather and brother are, you know."

She scoffed and stopped, turning to face him. "So you're telling me that you had no idea who I was. That your grandfather didn't tell you to get in my good graces and try to woo my land from me after your brother failed to get me to marry him?"

"I didn't know who you were until you told me your name." He rubbed his neck. "My grandfather did mention that he wanted me to talk to you."

Camille threw her hands in the air and started walking again.

He followed her. "Whatever was between us, wasn't a lie, Camille. You felt it as strongly as I did."

She rolled her eyes. "There is nothing between us, but dishonesty. You saw to that."

Silence hung thick behind her as she turned down Jenni's tree-lined street. Her chest tight, she fought the urge to look back. His footsteps crunched over the ground behind her again as he moved closer. She sighed.

"Look, Jer--" she screamed as she found herself upside down over his shoulder. "Put me down, you Neanderthal. I'm done talking to you."

He clamped one arm over her kicking legs and the other he used to swat her backside. Shocked, she froze at his blatant violation of her person. "Put me down," she bit out through clenched teeth.

He rubbed at the stinging spot on her backside as he muttered. "If you won't listen to me, I'll make you. Now be quiet."

Camille shrieked, pummeling his back with her fists. "You're just like the rest of your family, bullying and manhandling me to make me do what you want with no regard for my wishes."

Jeremy froze. Then he pulled her off his shoulder and set her down in front of him. She studied his clenched jaw and stricken gaze.

He stepped back from her. "I'm nothing like them. Nothing." He walked around to the passenger side door and opened it. "If someone broke into your house, then it might not be safe for you there. With your permission, I'll take you to Jenni's so you can get your car, then I'll follow you home and make sure the intruders didn't come back."

Biting her lip, Camille nodded and climbed silently up into the truck. He closed the door and came around to slide into the driver's seat. He put the truck in gear and drove the half-mile to Jenni's house, the tension between them thick enough to cut. She ignored the guilt urging her to apologize.

Jeremy pulled into the Pham drive. Camille glanced over at him, and then slid out of the truck. Her mind racing, she hurried inside and gathered her things from Jenni's room. She threw her bag into the passenger seat and pulled the car out of Jenni's driveway. His headlights, following behind her, confused her. Gary would have forced her into the truck, maybe even backhanded her into silence. Jeremy had seemed truly upset to be compared to the rest of his family.

They pulled up to her house. He followed her in silently and moved through each room of the house to be sure no one waited to do her harm. Camille found herself intrigued by his thoroughness.

He finished looking in the garage, and then moved back toward where she waited at the front door. "Everything looks clear. I checked all the windows."

Camille met his shuttered gaze. "I'm sorry."

Jeremy's startled gaze jerked up to meet hers. "For what?"

"For comparing you to your brother. He wouldn't have cared to check if the house was clear or the windows locked," she said, her eyes burning. "He'd have come in, stretched out on the couch and told me to get him a beer, food, or massage, if he'd bothered to stay at all."

Jeremy moved to stand in front of her. He closed his eyes and bent down to lean his forehead against hers. "You'll be the death of me, I can already tell."

Camille's stomach flipped. She pulled away from him even as her eyes found his lips. He was a Walker. He just wanted her land. This was all an act. But her heart wouldn't listen. He should have repulsed her, but she found herself leaning toward him. Her pulse pounded in her ears as he kissed her on the nose. Her startled gaze met his, confused.

He grimaced. "When I kiss you the first time, it will be because you want me to. I won't be accused of taking advantage of you."

Shocked by his restraint, Camille was even more shocked at the need to restrain herself. She felt a reluctant respect for this man, for a Walker. She imagined how she must appear to him and cringed. A line from her father's favorite book popped into her head. *You never really understand a person until you consider things from his point of view.*

He was her Boo Radley and she'd judged Jeremy just as harshly as Scout had Boo by assuming him to be as bad as his brother. She felt like a total dog biscuit. Her father read and discussed that book with her so many times. He'd have been so disappointed in her behavior. Her chest burned. She'd give anything to have him waiting at home to read it to her again. She caught her breath. That was it. The one word her father would have used that he knew she and no other would guess.

She knew the password. Mockingbird.

10

Camille gazed down at Jeremy, asleep on her couch, her mother's quilt draped over him. He'd asked to stay and she'd been secretly relieved. Though still attracted to him in the early morning light, Camille found herself suspicious of his motives. She believed that he hadn't known who she was at first, but she remembered the slip in his smile when she'd told him her name and his omission of his last name when he introduced himself.

Could she be in a relationship in which a lie, even one of omission, had already been told? She shook her head, torn, and moved past him to her father's office on silent, sock covered feet. She selected the much-used copy of *To Kill a Mockingbird* and took it along with her tablet to the window seat that looked over her mother's garden. She took the thumb drive from around her neck and inserted it into the tablet. When the security box appeared she carefully typed in mockingbird.

WRONG PASSWORD

Camille pressed her forehead against the window's glass as her stomach knotted. She'd been so sure. She picked up the book and opened the front cover, hoping for inspiration. It had to be something to do with this book. She fanned the pages. A slip of paper fell into her lap. She picked it up and unfolded it. A long sequence of numbers and letters, written in her father's neat hand, filled the paper.

Holding her breath, she typed the code.

WELCOME, CAMILLE.

Her heart rate accelerated. She clicked on the single file.

Inside were several documents, the top one labeled with her name.

She clicked on it.

My sweet Camille,

If you're reading this, then the unthinkable has happened. Whatever they tell you, please know that it is because of the information on this thumb drive that I am no longer with you and has nothing to do with the Walkers. (I know you've already jumped to that conclusion. Remember what Ms. Lee taught us, it's a sin to kill a mockingbird. Don't judge.) If Mr. Walker harasses you about the land, sell it to him. You can't afford the attention battling with him will bring. Keep the house if you can, but the land isn't worth your safety.

The first document lists everything I could learn about possible terrorist attacks blamed on Shines. I don't know when or how, but they are planning something big to turn ordinary people against you. The second document contains video of conversations between my boss, Brother Corey and a man he referred to only as The Reverend. I don't know much about the man, other than he considers Shines to be Satan spawn. Finally, the third document is a list of known or suspected Shines in Oklahoma. I've never been more thankful that we didn't take you to a doctor when your ability appeared. Delete this before you move on to the other files. We can't risk this falling into anyone else's hands.

I'm so proud of you, honey. You've always amazed me. Don't be ashamed to be a Shine. It's a gift from God. He gave it to you to use to glorify him. Don't let him down.

Remember Ms. Lee's words in Mockingbird. *Courage is not a man with a gun in his hand. It's knowing you're licked before you begin but you begin anyway and you see it through no matter what. You rarely win, but sometimes you do.*

I'm counting on you to make that "sometimes" happen. It's up to you now.

I love you.

Dad

The book slipped from her lap and hit the hard wood floor with a loud thump. Camille ignored it. Her eyes burned as she read the words again, refusing to blink. She'd always believed he wouldn't kill her mother and himself. Gentle hands on her shoulders made her look up, reminding her that she wasn't alone.

Jeremy bent down and retrieved her father's book. "What's wrong?"

"I found a note from my dad inside his favorite book," she said, laying the book over her tablet and the paper with the password.

Jeremy traced the embossed gold title of the leather bound book. "It's a sin to kill a mockingbird."

Her heart flipped. He'd zeroed in on the most special quote from the entire book. He even seemed to understand its symbolism. She moved her hand next to his on the book's cover, then leaned her forehead on his shoulder and sighed. "I don't know you, yet I feel as if I've been waiting for you my whole life. Is that weird?"

He laughed and rubbed the back of his neck. "As a matter of fact, it is, but I know exactly what you mean."

Camille looked up at him. She wanted to trust him, wanted to confide in him, but was afraid that until she knew his stance on Shines, she couldn't.

As if sensing her withdrawal, Jeremy smiled down at her then stood. "I think we both need to step back and think. You're obviously still dealing with your parents' deaths and I'm just returning from a six-year vacation from my family. Let's take it slow. Go out with me tonight. We'll do dinner, a movie, you know, things new couples often do on their first dates."

Camille nodded and stood. She clutched the book and tablet to her chest as she followed Jeremy to the front door. "Thank you for seeing me home last night and for staying to make sure the intruders didn't return."

He grabbed her hand, bent over it and kissed her knuckles as he'd done the night before. Camille rolled her eyes. He grinned. "Until tonight."

She closed the door and locked it behind him. He reached his truck, turned and caught her watching him. With a flourish of his hand, he gave her a deep bow more suited to an old world ballroom than her front yard and climbed into his truck. She shook her head, fighting a smile. She still couldn't believe she'd let another Walker into her house. The thought brought her father's words back to her and she leaned her forehead against the glass pane of the door. *It's a sin to kill a mockingbird.*

Her body shuddered as emotion overwhelmed her again. She replaced the paper with the password and returned to her father's office to place the book back on the shelf where it belonged. After making her way back to the window seat, she read the message from her father again.

She didn't want to delete the document, but knew she couldn't afford not to. Inhaling, she clenched her jaw, her finger hovering over delete file. Shaking her head, she closed the file. She'd do it later. Swallowing past the lump in her throat and shrugging away the guilt, she clicked on the first file. It contained a single list, cities from the United States and a few from various other countries.

Camille scanned the list. Seattle and Santa Monica were listed as the first two cities with New York City, Miami, and Dallas listed under them. Separated and in their own group were the foreign cities of Montreal, London, Rome, Cairo and Beijing. Highlighted below the list her father had typed one sentence.

Target cities. Shines will be blamed. How? For what purpose?

She caught her breath. Her parents had been killed before the Seattle tragedy. She minimized the file to click her browser icon and pull up a search engine. She quickly typed in Seattle and Shine, and then clicked on a national news site she recognized. She flashed hot then cold as an image of Seattle taken from the air appeared on the screen. She stared at the charred ruin. It looked as though a meteor had crashed in the center of the city forming a crater where once the famed space needle had been. The headline read-- SEATTLE DECIMATED BY SHINE

Camille clenched her jaw as she read about the first event to be blamed on Shines and the first city on her father's list. Returning to the search engine, she typed in Santa Monica and Shine. Again, the same periodical showed a picture of the devastation in that city. This time the Shine had died in the blast. She scrolled down the page as she read the article and found another image, one with three young women about her age all wearing the same pleated skirt and string-tie blouse. They were surrounded by an angry crowd. The headline read-- SHINES TO IDENTIFY SHINE RESPONSIBLE FOR SANTA MONICA INCIDENT

Aside from the blue hair of the first girl, they appeared normal. So normal that some cities were beginning to discuss detaining any young woman between the ages of fifteen and twenty-five. Camille closed out the browser window and stared down at the list of cities. Would New York be next? Her gut churned.

She clicked on the third file. A list of twenty names appeared. She hadn't known there were others like her. Halfway down the list, she froze and read the fifteenth name again unable to comprehend what she was seeing.

15. JENNIFER PHAM- 22 -Sentinel, OK

She sent the file to her printer. She closed the file, then removed the thumb drive and rubbed her finger over its shiny, black surface as her mind spun.

She'd known about the Shine incidents in Seattle and Santa Monica. Who hadn't? You couldn't turn on a television without having it rubbed constantly in your face. She'd even been dismayed with the pressure for the Senate to pass the bill nullifying Shines' rights upon discovery of a Shine, but it had been easy to distance herself from it all. Here in her sleepy corner of the world, it hadn't felt truly real. She'd done what she did best, stayed hidden. In the sanctuary her father had built for her, she'd been able to pretend it had nothing to do with her despite the growing anti-Shine movement growing in her own little town. Now, forced to sell her haven, she wouldn't have a hiding spot. Would they discover that she was Shine? And what about Jenni?

Camille squeezed the bridge of her nose between her fingers. She couldn't think about this right now. She'd hide the thumb drive with her Shine, then call Jenni. The soft brush of fabric was her only warning as something hard hit the side of her neck causing a flash of pain as everything went dark.

11

Camille regained consciousness to find both the thumb drive and her tablet gone. Head resting in one hand, she rubbed at her neck with the other. The pain in her head eased slowly until finally, she could lift her head without sunlight stabbing into her eyes. Slumped on the window seat, she leaned back against the cool glass of the window and lowered her shaking hand from her neck. Her emotions churned as she realized the letter was still on the thumb drive. She tightened her trembling fingers into a fist. She'd give anything to go back to the moment her emotions got the better of her and she refused to delete the letter. Her eyes burned. She'd just given herself away without using her Shine. Closing her eyes, she forced the helpless feeling drowning her, away.

The intruders would be working on extracting the information on the thumb drive. She didn't have time for a pity party. Pushing to her feet, she looked around her home. She couldn't stay here. Once they read the letter, they'd be back. Her eyes snagged on the paper waiting in the printer tray. She inhaled noisily. Jenny wasn't safe either. She grabbed the list of Shines from the printer, packed her car with her clothes and most cherished possessions, then drove to Jenni's house. Fear was a sick churning in her stomach.

She forced a smile when Jenni opened the door. "We need to talk." She thrust the paper into her best friend's hands.

Jenni scanned the sheet and her faced paled. "Where did you get this?"

41

"The thumb drive, right before I was knocked out and it was stolen."

Jenni swayed and put her hand on the entry hall wall.

Camille moved past her and took the stairs to the second floor. "Why didn't you tell me?"

"The same reason you never came out and said anything to me. The information is dangerous."

Camille waited for Jenni to follow her into the bedroom, then closed the door. "We aren't safe here anymore. There was a letter on the thumb drive from my father. I didn't delete it before they took the thumb drive. Both of us have been compromised." Camille looked away from her friend's accusing eyes. "You were right. We should have destroyed it when we had the chance."

Jenni sat heavily on the bed. "It wouldn't have mattered for me. If you're father found that list, then someone else put it together. It was just a matter of time until they came for me."

"The Shine events in Seattle and Santa Monica weren't the fault of Shines. The government set us up. My father found as much information as he could and left it for me in the thumb drive. My parents died because he knew that information." A tear trailed down her cheek as she sat next to Jenni. "My parents' deaths were my fault."

Jenni put an arm around her shoulders and pulled her in for a hug. "Not true. Whether you'd been Shine or not, your father would have worked where he did and discovered what he did. The people he learned the information from were to blame." Jenni sat up and wiped the tear from Camille's cheek.

Her hands, sweaty moments before were dry and her whole body felt cooler. Camille eyed her friend. "You control temperature somehow."

Jenni shrugged and smiled. "I'm really good at warming

up icy feet." The spark of humor in her eyes dimmed. "We can't let them win. We need more information and a plan."

They spent the day looking at everything they could find on the Seattle and Santa Monica Shine events. Jenni's brow wrinkled as she stared at the photo of the three women in uniforms, Camille had seen in her earlier search. Running her fingers over the screen, Jenni enlarged the picture trying to read the crest on the uniforms. It was a light house shining amidst the dark clouds of a stormy sky. Under the lighthouse were words written in what looked to be Latin.

Jenni enlarged it again. "What does Commutans Lux Vestra mean?"

Camille opened up another window and pulled up a language translator. She typed in the words and read. "Changing your light." She snorted and closed the window. "The rehab center those women are being held in put that on there for sure."

Jenni ran her finger along the image of the lighthouse. "This is what we're meant to be. A light guiding the world during dark times with our gifts, not pariahs being hunted and changed by the government." She shrunk the image back to its original size. "We have to help each other or this is going to be the future for all of us."

Camille threw herself back onto Jenni's bed. "Do you know how your name could be on this list?" She looked over at her friend as Jenni stood to pace beside the bed.

"My parents took me to a Vietnamese doctor in the city when my Shine first appeared. I've no way of knowing who the doctor spoke to about it." Jenni said, as she turned and opened her closet.

Jenni pulled a large empty suitcase from the back of her closet and hoisted it up on the bed beside Camille.

"What're you doing?"

Jenni glanced her way as she started taking clothes from the closet. "We can't stay, Cam. They'll lock us up like those other women. We have to become the lighthouse for others like us. To do that, we need to leave and start gathering others like us."

Camille's heart pounded in her chest. "What about your father? Michael?"

Jenni stopped, her chin on her chest as her shoulders sunk. "My father and I have spoken about this. We knew the possibility existed that the SSS or the government could discover my existence and come for me." Jenni turned and pulled a small locked box from the top of her closet. "I barely know Michael. He'll forget me and move on when it's clear I'm gone for good."

Jenni opened the box and Camille's eyes widened at the stack of hundreds and twenties as Jenni transferred them to a blue zippered pouch lying at the bottom of the box.

A lump formed in her throat. This was really happening. Her chest burned. She released the breath she held. This was her fault. If she'd never found that thumb drive, it couldn't have been stolen. Her home would still be safe.

She rubbed her neck where the thief had hit her. She still had a slight headache from the ordeal. She glanced up as her friend returned to the bed to place more clothing into the suitcase. Seeing the tears glisten on her friend's cheek, Camille realized how selfish she was being. Her face burned. She stood and opened her arms. Jenni's face crumpled as she stepped into Camille's embrace. Her friend was leaving the only home she'd ever known, a man who could have been her soulmate and her only family.

"I'm having difficulty understanding God's plan in this. I don't want to be on the run for the rest of my life, always wondering if the SSS or the government will discover where I'm hiding. My father is old. He planned to retire as soon as Michael felt ready to take over. I should be here caring for him."

Camille made soothing sounds as she rubbed her friend's back, her own tears flowing. Where would they go? How would they manage without giving themselves away? They would need jobs. The rest of Camille's savings and Jenni's money would only last so long.

She shuddered. Maybe Jenni could hide at her place until this blew over. Surely, her father's copy of the list hadn't been the only one. If they'd wanted to gather up those Shines, they'd have come for Jenni before now.

"Maybe we're being too hasty. The list on the thumb drive couldn't have been the only one. My father had to have gotten it from somewhere. If they'd wanted you, they could have come for you at any time."

Jenni pulled away from Camille, her brow furrowed in thought as she pulled up the bottom of her t-shirt to dry her face. "We don't know who it was that took the thumb drive. This may be God's way of telling us we need to fight against what's being done to us." Camille opened her mouth to protest, but Jenni shook her head and held up a hand. "We can't hide forever. If none of us stand up and fight back, we might as well walk right up to the SSS or one of the government's rehab facilities and turn ourselves in. You and I can become the lighthouse that guide's others like us to a safe harbor. They can't be allowed to change who we are, Cam. It's up to us, don't you see?"

"Can two people really fight back against the government?" Camille asked, wrapping her arms around herself.

Jenni pulled her shoulders back, her eyes filling with determination. "Not alone, but there are others like us. If we find them and join together, maybe we stand a chance."

Jenni grabbed the list Camille had printed. "We'll start by finding them."

Camille nodded and began searching the net for the names on her list. She admired her friend's courage. Camille didn't want to be a hero. She simply wished to find a new safe haven and hide.

12

Jenni's father returned from work and Camille called Jeremy about their date. She'd wanted to give the Phams privacy as they discussed the implications of what Camille had discovered on the thumb drive.

Now she sat in Jeremy's truck as he pulled up to a pond surrounded by trees that sat on his family property. Camille's heart threatened to pound itself right out of her chest as Jeremy helped her out of his truck. It was going to be a perfect first date. She glanced shyly at him and froze. He stood in a bright shaft of sunlight, his eyes sparkling a bright blue as he smiled over at her. Her heart fluttered in her chest. This was such a bad idea. All the reasons she shouldn't be here circled in her head. She shoved aside her doubts and followed him toward the pond. Rays of sunlight filtered between tree branches to dance on the water like fairies playing tag. She smiled. She'd have the memory, if nothing else.

"This place is beautiful."

He smiled. "A picnic at my favorite place on God's Earth seemed like just the spot for our first date."

A blanket lay spread across the ground with a low camp table set beside it holding a bottle of wine in a bucket of ice, two unlit candles in their holders and a picnic basket. A small speaker attached to an mp3 player played soft piano music.

Camille smiled. The soothing notes of "Moonlight Sonata" were one of her favorites. "Beethoven? You surprise me, Mr. Walker."

He led her to the blanket. "I enjoy instrumentals when I

need to think or don't want the intrusiveness of music with words."

She lowered herself to the blanket as he pulled two glasses, a cork screw and a plastic wrapped plate of cheese, meat, and bread from the basket.

"This is exactly what I needed. It's been a long day and tomorrow promises to be longer," she said, taking the glass of Chardonnay he held out to her.

She took a drink, allowing the acidic liquid to sit in her mouth as she closed her eyes and savored the flavor. The birds and Beethoven played in the background. Yes, she'd needed this moment of perfect peace before the storm building on her horizon broke.

The sound of plastic wrap pulled her mind from the troubling thoughts trying to intrude. She opened her eyes. Jeremy pulled the plastic from the plate and balled it up, shooting it like a basketball into the picnic basket. Camille reached for a piece of the cheddar and realized he'd paired the wine and cheese perfectly. She smiled. A man after her own heart.

"What's that smile about?" he asked, eyebrow lifted.

Camille's happiness evaporated as reality, ever ready to pounce, crept back into her thoughts. "You can pair wine and cheese. Why couldn't I have met you earlier?"

Jeremy leaned in closer. "That sounds almost like regret in your voice, but we're here now. The future is wide open."

Camille glanced away from his penetrating gaze. "My immediate future doesn't have a place for a serious relationship right now, if it ever will."

She glanced back and he winked at her. "God has an amazing sense of humor. When it's meant to be, He sees that it works itself out, even when you think there's no way it could."

Camille rolled her eyes. "If God thinks being forced to sell my home because my dad is accused of the murder of my mother and his own suicide that voids the life insurance is funny, then God is not the kind, loving God my mother taught me about."

Jeremy's smile faded as he covered her hand with his own and squeezed. "That wasn't God, Camille and you know it. Humans are given the freedom to make our own choices and most of the time we choose terribly." He leaned forward, so that their breaths mingled. "What's important is that you're here and I'm here. There's the potential for something great between us, if you're brave enough to give it a go."

Camille closed her eyes against his penetrating gaze and struggled to breathe through the pressure building in her chest. Why couldn't she have met him in another life when she wasn't plagued by her Shine and the world's view of it? Manic laughter threatened to spill from her throat, but she pressed her lips together to hold it in. Maybe she should tell him about her Shine. He wouldn't be so keen on exploring their potential then.

Swallowing the lump in her throat, Camille opened her eyes. "Jenni and I have a long road trip planned. I'm not sure when we'll return. You'd do better to find someone else to explore potential with."

Jeremy frowned. "A road trip? Like a vacation? When are you leaving? How long do you plan to be gone?"

She shrugged and wrapped her arms around herself. "It's something we've been planning. We want to travel while we're both still single and don't have families." She bit her lip. "We leave tomorrow."

"What? For how long?" he asked, incredulous.

Camille stared at the pond as something from beneath the surface caused ripples to disturb its smooth surface.

"We haven't decided. Depends on what we find."

Jeremy stood and began to pace, disrupting her view of the pond. "So you'll be gone a couple weeks? A month? All summer?"

She glanced up at him. "We don't know." He stopped pacing with his back to her and stared out over the pond. Camille lifted her eyebrows. The peace of the date had been very short lived. Camille stood. "Look, this was great, but maybe you should take me back to Jenni's house."

He swung around, face set as he moved toward her. He stopped inches from her, their eyes locked. He lifted his hand and tucked the hair blowing across her face behind her ear. Camille shuddered as his finger brushed her cheek. Her eyes lowered to his mouth. His hands cupped her face as he leaned down and covered her mouth with his. Camille wrapped her arms around his neck and closed her eyes as heat moved from her lips, down her body.

Lost in the sensation of his hard lips and his harder body, Camille moaned. He pulled back. She opened her eyes. "You shouldn't have done that."

"It's real, Camille. I've never felt like this over one kiss in my life. Every time we're together, it feels as though a current of electricity is running under my skin." He inhaled loudly. "You feel it too, I know you do."

Camille stepped back. "We shouldn't do that again. I'm leaving. Tell your grandfather I'm willing to sell so long as it's another iodine mine and not that women's rehab facility being built on my land."

Jeremy's eyes flashed. "My grandfather can hang for all I care. I didn't bring you here to entice your land from you."

"I know, but my life doesn't have room for a relationship right now." She made her voice go cold. She had to push him away for his own good. "I'm willing to sell, but I need to finalize everything in the morning. I assume your grandfather has the money sitting ready in some fat bank account. Tell him to meet me at the bank when it opens tomorrow morning."

He clenched his jaw and turned away from her. Camille bent down and began to return everything to the picnic basket.

"Leave it. I'll take you back to Jenni's and come back later."

Camille cringed inside, but kept her face carefully blank. She stood and walked to his truck in silence. It had to be this way. Inside her heart broke into a million pieces for what could have been.

13

Camille paced near the bank's entrance, ignoring the busy traffic filling the town's main street. She'd packed all her personal family photo albums, mementos, and important files into three large boxes and stored them in Jenni's attic, marked with her name. She hoped Dr. Pham wouldn't mind holding them for her until a day when she could return for them.

She kept out only a few pictures and her mother's jewelry, which she had stuffed into one of two large suitcases with her clothes and placed into the trunk of her mom's old Honda. She'd been sad to leave her vintage Volkswagen Beetle, but knew its bright red color and unique shape would only attract attention they didn't need. Her mother's Honda wouldn't be noticed no matter where they went. It was shocking to realize how little she truly needed from the home she'd grown up in.

She checked her watch again. Where was Jenni? She'd spoken to her friend a couple of hours before. They'd agreed to meet at the bank so they could leave as soon as she'd finished signing the deed over to Jeremy's grandfather. The old man had already been here, taken the deed, paid her and left. Jeremy hadn't come. She'd ignored her disappointment. What right did she have to expect anything else from him?

She left most of her money in her savings account, knowing that to withdraw such a large amount would garner too much attention. She'd added Jenni and Dr. Pham's names to her accounts after her parents' deaths since they were her only family. The tragedy had taught her you could never be too prepared.

Wondering where her friend could be, Camille again cursed the theft of her tablet. She glanced at her watch. Her stomach churned. Something wasn't right. Jenni should have been here thirty minutes ago. She glanced up the town's main street, buzzing with weekday morning business, but didn't see any sign of Jenni or her little white electric car.

The prickle of unease intensified. Jenni didn't change her mind, ever. If she wasn't here, something was wrong. Camille jumped in her car and raced to Jenni's house. As she turned down the street, her unease became alarm. A large black car, back windows tinted black, pulled away from the house.

She slowed her car to get a good look at the driver and slammed on her brakes. She recognized that square jaw and military haircut. The male intruder she'd hit with the shoe. She looked at the person sitting in the passenger seat, sure it'd be a woman, and stopped breathing. Gary, looking behind him into the backseat, sat next to the man in the car. Camille hit the gas. Why was Gary with the intruder? Had she been wrong to think the Walker's had nothing to do with the break-ins? Had Jeremy lied to her? She remembered the black car had been pulling away from Jenni's and had to wipe her clammy hands on her pant leg. Why had they been at Jenni's and where was her friend?

14

Camille swung into the Phams' drive with a screech of tires. The garage door was open and two large suitcases sat beside the opened hatch back of Jenni's car. Camille threw her car in park, jumped out, and ran into the house.

"Jenni? Dr. Pham?" she yelled.

She strained her ears, but the house remained silent. She raced through the utility room and into the kitchen. One of the dining room chairs was missing. Another chair lay overturned on the floor next to Jenni's large purse. Heart pounding, she passed into the living room and froze.

Her voice, a strained whisper, shook as she called out to Dr. Pham where he sat, tied to the missing dining chair, his head slumped over onto his chest. "Dr. Pham?"

She knelt next to the chair and placed her hand over his chest. Tears pricked her eyes as the reassuring beat of his heart thumped under her hand. She picked at the knots in the rope until they fell loose and she could pull them from his body. Grabbing him with a hand under each arm, she half carried, half dragged him to the couch and laid him down, noticing the lump on the back of his head. She ran into the kitchen and grabbed a bag of frozen spinach from the freezer and a hand towel then placed them so that the spinach lay between the bump on his head and the couch.

The older man moaned and his eyelids fluttered, but didn't open. He mumbled Jenni's name and Camille jumped up. Jenni! She ran up the stairs, knowing she'd find no one up there. Gary had been looking into the backseat at someone and Camille had a feeling she knew exactly who he'd been looking at. The door to Jenni's room was busted as if someone had kicked it open. Had Jenni locked herself inside? Camille rushed into Jenni's room to find the usually immaculate space, a shambles. The bedspread was gone, the sheets were twisted on the bed. The knick-knacks on the dresser lay on their sides or were scattered on the floor around it. The bedside table drawer hung open, Jenni's tablet in it.

Camille picked up the tablet. Her friend wouldn't have left it here, she'd have had it with her when she left to meet Camille. She'd probably had it in her hand as she walked through the dining room with her purse when Jeremy and the others in the black car had arrived. They'd probably come in through the garage and surprised her. She'd rushed up here, locked the door, and...what?

Camille turned on the tablet and entered her friend's password. The yellow page of the notebook program appeared, two sentences, the last unfinished, filled the top of the page.

They've come for me. Don't trust Jeremy!

Camille sat on the bed, tears streaming down her face, unsure what to do. Where would they have taken her? The Shine Rehab Reservation in Arapaho, two hours away? Camille rushed out of the room and down the stairs, slowing as she noticed Dr. Pham pushing himself up to a sitting position. She sat beside him on the couch.

"Keep this pressed to your head. It'll help with the swelling."

The old man took the cold pack from her and leaned back against the couch, resting the back of his head on it. "Jenni?" His voice sounded tired.

"They took her." Camille leaned forward. "Dr. Pham, did they say anything to indicate where they might be taking her?"

Dr. Pham shook his head. "No, but they said Brother Corey will be only too happy to take credit for her acquisition with the Reverend, whatever that means."

"Brother Corey?" Camille shot to her feet. Brother Corey had been her dad's boss. She didn't think it was just a coincidence.

15

Camille tapped her foot as Michael parked his truck down a neighborhood side street a short distance from the church. He'd pulled up in his truck just as she'd stepped out of the Phams' house. She'd wanted so badly to call Jeremy, but Jenni's note had said not to trust him. Was Jeremy part of this with his brother? Had telling him their plans to leave prompted the abduction?

Knowing she couldn't do this alone and realizing secrets wouldn't do her any good, she had told Michael everything except what Jenni had said about trusting Jeremy. She didn't want to believe that he'd be involved. They decided that the church was the most likely place Gary would have taken Jenni and headed straight here.

The black car was nowhere to be seen, but Camille wasn't surprised. Behind the over-sized gray building, a huge garage housed the church's vehicles. The black car, no doubt, sat inside it.

"Do you think she's in there?" Michael asked, his voice low as if he thought they'd hear them from here.

Camille nodded, studying the building that had once housed a big box hardware store. "This place is huge and has plenty of empty rooms where they could hide her until they are ordered to move her someplace more permanent. And they could slip her inside through the garage without anyone seeing them."

"How do we get inside?"

She opened the truck's door and climbed out. "It's a church. The doors are always open during the day."

Michael walked around the truck to stand beside her. "So we're just going to walk inside?"

Camille let a small smile lift the corners of her lips.

"Unfortunately, I don't have the ability to teleport us."

Michael glanced at her, eyebrows lifted. "There's a Shine that does?"

She shrugged. "I don't have any idea, really, but wouldn't it be razor if there was?"

A red convertible pulled into the parking lot, holding three men and a woman. Camille recognized them as the worship leader and his team. Their ticket in. She closed her eyes and relaxed control of her Shine, allowing it to broadcast her order to keep them invisible. The voices of the worship team exiting the shiny red convertible reached her ears.

When she was sure the command reached as far as her mind could broadcast, she opened her eyes and stepped forward, brushing Michael's arm.

He glanced down, and then swung around. "Camille?"

"Keep your voice down." Camille rolled her eyes as Michael tentatively reached toward the sound of her voice. "Welcome to my world."

"You're invisible." Eyes wide, a smile stretched across his face. "That's amazing."

She reached out and grabbed his arm. "No one can see either of us. Come on."

"You can make me invisible, too?"

Camille pulled him toward the worship leader. "They can still hear us. Step carefully. Don't talk. We'll follow them in so our entrance isn't noticed."

"It'd be easier if I could still see you," he whispered.

Camille stopped and he collided with her. Used to keeping her Shine tightly under her control, she nearly stopped the pulsing in her brain. Remembering her mission, she concentrated on it until she had it securely locked into place again. She'd never tried to separate who she affected with her power. Could it be done? She shook her head. The worship group was almost to the doors. Yanking Michael's arm, she rushed to catch up.

"If we get separated, we'll meet back at your truck." Camille whispered over her shoulder as the group opened the church's doors and began to file inside. The woman pulling up the rear glanced over her shoulder and shrugged. Camille squeezed Michael's hand.

They slipped inside. She pulled Michael to the side opposite the direction of the worship team. They were in a large open area. A welcome counter stood directly across from them with the doors to the children's area to the left and a wide hallway, which the worship team was traveling through, in the center. To the far right, the hospitality area stood empty and ready for the next service and the army of volunteers who would serve the many guests that walked through these doors each weekend.

Camille's father used to slip her behind the counter when she was a child and let her help serve donuts, fruit, coffee, tea, and water each morning before their usual service. She'd loved helping. Brother Corey had no business bringing the SSS into her church. She clenched her jaw. She'd get her friend back first, and then she'd make sure to somehow clue the main campus in Oklahoma City to this one's duplicity.

Tugging Michael's arm, she pulled him toward the doors to the children's area. It would be deserted this time of the week, making it the best place to hide someone. Glancing around to make sure they weren't being watched by the lady at the welcome counter, Camille opened the door and slipped through, making sure to hold it as it closed. The click as it shut echoed down the hallway. Camille cringed.

They stood in a long, wide hall lined with doors, most open, their rooms dark.

Michael brushed against her arm. "What's the plan?"

Camille shrugged, then remembered he couldn't see her. She wished she'd thought to test out her ability to pick and choose who she affected with her power.

"Check the rooms with closed doors on that side, I'll do the same on this side."

They made their way down the hallway, the click of doors opening and closing the only sound. When they came to an intersecting hall, Camille froze. Gary, accompanied by the man with the crooked nose who'd broken into her house and the woman who'd helped break into her house filed out of one of the rooms, giving Camille a glimpse of Jenni huddled in a cage.

The woman, voice devoid of warmth, pulled the door shut and turned to Gary and Crooked Nose. "Was zapping her that hard really necessary?"

Gary and Crooked Nose laughed and rolled their eyes. "Hard learned lessons are the best lessons. We don't have to worry about her trying to escape again, do we?"

The woman shrugged as they filed toward a set of clear glass doors at the end of the hallway. Camille waited three heartbeats after they disappeared out the doors before she grabbed Michael's arm and approached the room holding her friend.

"Let me go in first," Michael whispered. "We can't afford to have something happen to you, if we want out of this building."

Unease slid down Camille's back as the doorknob turned in Michael's hand. They were so confident Jenni wouldn't escape, they didn't even bother to lock the door?

She tugged on Michael's arm. "Careful."

Michael eased the door open. The large room held a row of five connected rectangular cages. Jenni lay huddled near the door of the first cage, tears leaking from her closed eyes. A flat band of silver metal circled her head, an athlete's clear mouthpiece attached to it. Jenni's jaw clamped the mouthpiece so hard, the muscles in her neck and face stood out.

Camille studied her friend. No ropes, chains, or manacles kept Jenni from standing and using her power to melt the lock on the door, yet she huddled frozen on the floor within reaching distance of the lock. Camille glared at the metal band that had something to do with her friend's incapacitation.

They eased over to Jenni's cage. Reaching through the bars, Camille whispered. "Hold perfectly still, I'm going to try to get this thing off of you."

Jenni's eyes popped open, a keening sound in her throat as she jerked her head away from Camille's voice and loosened her jaw. "Don't."

Camille froze. Jenni's body arched, her eyes rolling back in her head as the hairs on Camille's arm lifted. The band was some type of electrical device. But what triggered it?

Michael swore as Jenni's body relaxed, more tears leaking from her eyes. Her friend breathed noisily through her nose and through her teeth clenched on the mouthpiece.

"How is it triggered?" she asked Jenni who simply squeezed her eyes shut, a slight tremor in her body.

"How do we get it off of her?" Michael asked. "It seems to be triggered by movement."

Camille studied the device. "It's triggered by her movement, but someone had to put it on her and will eventually have to pull it off."

Jenni's eyes popped open again. She shook her head. Her body arched, her heels drumming the floor.

Michael cursed again. "We have to get it off of her."

As Jenni's body relaxed, Camille reached for the device.

Camille's fingers touched the metal band and her hand went numb as an electrical current ran under her skin like a stream of hot, thick water threatening to burst her veins. Stars exploded in her mind as the current hit her brain like a lightning bolt, freezing every muscle in place. Michael's eyes widened, his mouth moving, but Camille's eyes rolled up in her head as her body reflexively jerked back and crumpled on the floor.

When the current stopped, Camille lay panting on the floor, every muscle in her body bruised. Before she could reassure Michael that she was okay, the door banged open behind them. Camille slowly turned her head as Michael jumped to his feet and spun around. Gary, Crooked Nose, and the woman stood in the door, guns pointed at them. With a sinking heart, she realized the electricity hitting her brain had frozen her occipital lobe causing her Shine to stop working.

16

Gary and Crooked Nose shoved Michael into the middle cage, while the woman moved Camille into a third cage and placed another of the bands on her head. She glared at Gary until her burning eyes forced her to blink. Electricity shot through her, making her heart swell in her chest and threatened to beat a hole through her sternum. When the thick water sensation once again subsided, Camille locked her muscles in place afraid to open her eyes, afraid to even breathe very deeply for fear the movement of her lungs would set it off again.

Michael rattled the bars of his cage. "You have to get those off of them. Their hearts are going to be seriously damaged if they're electrocuted too many more times."

Gary's voice shot across the room. "I wouldn't have pegged you for a Shine puppet, Saunders. You're a God fearing man. Don't you realize what abominations these Shine are? Join us. Tell us what you know of the Ohm. God will shower you with blessings for your loyalty and faithfulness against these daughters of Satan."

Michael snorted. "You're insane, Walker. God gave these women these gifts. Like the rest of the SSS, you're just jealous you weren't chosen."

"You'll burn in hell for that, heretic, and the Reverend will make you pay before you get there." Camille recognized the raspy voice of Crooked Nose as he yelled at Michael.

"Both of you shut up." the woman yelled. "The Reverend will enjoy getting every secret of the Ohm and its location out of you. You'll wish you'd never left the safety of the California desert and your Shine masters."

"You and your Reverend will both be disappointed then, because I don't know what an Ohm is and I've never even been to the California desert," Michael growled through clenched teeth.

She heard surprise in Gary's voice. "Why would you help two Shines if you weren't a puppet of the Shine Resistance?"

Michael gave a bark of humorless laughter. "Because it's the right thing to do. Unlike you, I'm not afraid of what I don't understand."

They moved away from the cages. She heard footsteps pause. "Whether you know of the Ohm and its location or not, it's too late for you. You really shouldn't have involved yourself."

The door closed and a thick tension descended on the room as both Jenni and Camille held themselves frozen, their shallow breathing loud in the silence.

Michael shifted closer to her in his cage. "Camille, if you can hear and understand me, hold your breath for a second. Camille complied and Michael sighed. "If I can get out of here, I can go get my dad. Can you use your Shine on me again?"

Sweat trickled down her temple and between her breasts as her heart pounded in her chest. She could make him invisible, but he'd still be stuck in that cage. Trusting that he knew what he was doing, she braced herself for the jolt of electricity afraid the pulsing of her occipital lobe would send electricity coursing through her once again. She sighed when it didn't.

She pushed the command that no one would see Michael as far as she could, a headache pounding at her temples. All she could do was wait and hope that she didn't get zapped again before Michael escaped and could get to his father for help.

The sound of the door opening sent her heart into overdrive. She forced herself to keep taking noisy, shallow breaths through her nose. A shout filled the room as Crooked Nose realized the middle cage was empty.

"He escaped." She heard him pull on the door to Michael's cage. "And the door is still locked."

The sound of the lock disengaging nearly made her forget and open her eyes, but she locked every muscle and stayed still. The cage's door opened and Crooked Nose muttered as he inspected the cell for how Michael could have escaped.

Gary's voice sounded from the room's door. "We need to search the building. He's here somewhere."

Crooked Nose's boots echoed on the tile floor as he followed the woman and Gary out of the room, the door slamming behind him. Silence descended on the room, the sounds of Jenni and Camille's shallow breaths the only sound. Camille strained her ears, listening for Michael.

"Thank you, Camille," Michael whispered. "I'll be back with help."

The quiet swishing sound of cloth was the only evidence that Michael moved across the room. The sound paused as he must have stopped to listen. The door opened with a rush of air, then a soft click as it closed. Jenni and Camille continued to breathe shallowly, both praying Michael would return before Gary decided to move them.

17

Every muscle in Camille's body hurt from staying still so long. A spot on her left leg threatened to drive her insane if she didn't get to scratch it soon. Her muscles trembled and sweat dampened the back of her shirt. They'd been in here, frozen and alone, for what felt like hours.

Camille screamed her frustration silently in her mind. She felt trapped in a deprivation tank behind the darkness of her closed eyelids, with only her and Jenni's shallow breathing for company. She'd spent the last hour counting Jenni's breaths. At thirty-six hundred breaths, the exact number of seconds in an hour, she'd stopped and stilled her Shine, hoping Michael had time to get out.

The door of the room opened and she silently sighed. Finally. A wave of cinnamon scented air filled her nose as two sets of footsteps moved into the room, their steps different than either the woman or Crooked Nose. Camille waited, but no one spoke. Her heart rate picked up. Who could it be? The footsteps moved toward Jenni's cage as another set of footsteps, boots by the sound, clicked across the tile from the door.

Pages rustled. "Jennifer Pham, twenty-two, has lived in Sentinel her entire life. She was taken to an Asian doctor in Oklahoma City at the age of twelve after she cooled a fever in a dog brought to her father's veterinary clinic with the touch of her hand. The doctor's records also noted that she'd placed her hands on her father and increased his body temperature when he mentioned being cool, nearly giving him a heat stroke prompting the trip to the doctor,"

Jeremy's familiar voice reported.

Camille jerked and cried out as the skin on her neck burned, then a wave of electricity zipped through her body like thick molasses, swelling her veins, filling her heart to bursting. When the current subsided, tears leaked from Camille's eyes. Her heart, thumping rapidly, sat bruised in her chest. The trembling in her muscles increased as she breathed shallowly, desperate for a deep breath to ease the pounding headache from lack of oxygen.

The unknown set of footsteps moved toward her cage, followed by Jeremy's boots. "Camille Leon, twenty-three, has lived in Sentinel her entire life. Close friends with Miss Pham, we only recently learned from the thumb drive Drew and Eve retrieved that she has Shine ability, though we still don't know what her Shine might be."

The voice belonging to the unknown footsteps was warm and filled with approval. "Excellent job, Mr. Walker. You prove that my regard is well placed."

"You honor me, Reverend," Jeremy said, voice soft.

So this was the esteemed Reverend. If she'd been able to move she'd have let him know exactly what she thought of him and those like him. Fuming, she could only listen.

The Reverend moved closer to her cage. "I regret that this location has been compromised. I find myself curious to discover Miss Leon's Shine and how she eluded our notice for so long." He turned abruptly and moved back to the door. "Is the new location ready?"

The click of Jeremy's boots followed the Reverend to the room's door. "As we speak, Reverend."

"Good. The Sheriff can't be allowed to discover any evidence that we were ever here."

"He will find nothing." Jeremy assured the older man.

The Reverend paused in the doorway. "You're sure the Sheriff's boy knew nothing of the Ohm?"

"He thought the Ohm was an object when we mentioned it. Knowing the man his whole life, I'm inclined to believe him. He swore he'd never been to the California desert and since he went to university at Oklahoma State in Stillwater, I doubt he's even been out of the state."

"Very well, then. Carry on with evacuations. I'll meet you at the new location." The Reverend's steps echoed down the hall, but Jeremy's boots remained still.

A bitter taste filled Camille's mouth as Jeremy's boots moved back to her cage and stopped. The thought of him simply staring at her, stabbed at her heart. She couldn't believe she'd fallen for him, actually believed they had a real connection. He was worse than his brute of a brother.

Fabric rustled as Jeremy crouched down near her cage and whispered. "It's a sin to kill a mockingbird."

Heat crawled up her neck as she forced herself to bite the mouthpiece in her mouth tighter. How dare he mock her. How dare he sully those cherished words with his voice. She longed to scratch his eyes out.

He stood and his boots moved to the room's door where he paused. "Look beyond the surface, Camille. Things aren't always what they seem."

Her stomach churned. What did he mean? She was in a cage and he had put her there. How else was she supposed to see it?

18

Camille sat stiffly in a black SUV, Jeremy beside her with a hand taser pressed into her side. Only the lights from the door panels and the front console lit the interior. Afternoon had passed and the sun set while they'd been trapped in the church. Had Michael made it to his father? Jenny sat in the seat behind her, Gary holding a taser to her friend's side.

"You're scum," she said, glaring out the corner of her eye at Jeremy. "I hope the Ohm finds you and makes you pay for hunting Shines."

A squeal sounded from behind her and she could feel a vibration in her seat as if someone kicked the back of her seat rapidly.

"Damn it, Gary, stop." Jeremy said, glaring over his shoulder.

Camille turned her head to look over her shoulder to see Gary glaring at her. "She opens her yap again, and I'll taser her little friend again."

Jeremy snorted in disgust and turned back to the front, pressing the taser harder into Camille's side. "For her sake, you'd better keep quiet."

Camille glanced at her shaking friend as Jenni slumped in her seat, her desperate eyes meeting Camille's as if pleading for her to stay quiet. Camille faced the front once again, her hands clenched in her lap.

Jeremy met and held her gaze, his hand gently squeezing her arm. She narrowed her eyes and jerked her arm away from him. Jeremy sighed then leaned toward Crooked Nose in the driver's seat when he muttered his name over his shoulder.

Something slammed into the back of the SUV with a loud crunch. Camille found herself jerked to the side as Gary flew over her seat and crashed into the back of Jeremy.

"What the--," Jeremy shoved his brother back over his seat. "Buckle your seat belt before they h--"

The other vehicle hit them again, sending the back of the SUV sliding until it was sideways on the road. Jeremy pointed out Camille's window. "Watch out."

An oncoming diesel hit the front of the SUV and Camille was jerked forward against her seat belt. The SUV spun across the two-lane highway, sliding up onto two wheels before rolling down the embankment. Jeremy wrapped his arms around her, forcing her head into the crook of his neck as the vehicle rolled end over end down a steep embankment and glass shattered.

Jenni screamed behind her. "Camille."

When the vehicle stopped, Camille hung upside down in her seatbelt feeling as though she'd been beaten with a two by four, Jeremy's arms still tight around her.

Jeremy ran his hands over her body. "You okay."

"Get off me," she bit out, hitting the release on her seatbelt and falling to the SUV's roof.

"Camille--" Jeremy started, but voices shouted outside the vehicle, silencing him.

"Help," she screamed. "Please, help me."

She scrambled under the back of her seat, seeing no evidence of Gary. She ran trembling hands over Jenni who hung limp from her own seatbelt. Holding her breath, Camille felt for Jenni's pulse and sighed in relief as the first face appeared at the SUV's shattered window.

"Everyone okay in there?" a woman, dressed all in black, asked, using her sleeve to clear the jagged shards of shattered glass from the window's frame.

Camille patted Jenni on the cheek, wanting to wake her, but afraid to move her in case she was injured. "Jenni, wake up."

Her friend's eyes fluttered as she moaned. "Camille?"

"Can you move? Turn your head for me."

Jenni turned her head and pulled her arms and legs into her body. "I think I'm okay. Just bruised, but nothing serious."

Camille reached for her friend's seatbelt release. "I'm going to release your safety belt. Get ready. Now."

Jenni dropped to the SUV's roof and surged into Camille's arms. "Oh Cam, I thought we were dead for sure."

Camille pulled her friend toward the woman whispering to Jeremy at the window. "Don't believe anything he says. We were taken against our will. Please help us."

The woman glanced toward Jeremy and nodded. A chill crawled down her back. Was this another one of them?

She pushed Jenni toward the window and leaned in close to her ear. "As soon as we clear the window, run for it. Meet back here when they stop searching for us."

A barely perceptible nod--Jenni's only response-- reassured Camille. Jenni crawled out first, then Camille rushed out after her breaking into a run as soon as she got to her feet. She had the command ready and released control of her Shine.

Jeremy's voice yelled after her. "Camille, wait." But she ignored him and ran as fast and as far as she could into a field full of almost ripe wheat. Shot's fired behind them as Gary limped into the SUV's upside down headlights, gun firing in their direction.

She slammed to a halt as Jenni screamed in pain behind her. More shots sounded. Gary's body bowed backwards and he collapsed to the ground. Camille didn't have time to wonder where the shots came from. Her friend lay in the wheat somewhere behind her, possibly bleeding to death.

Camille ducked into the wheat and called in a loud whisper. "Jenni. Where are you?"

"Here." Jenni's weak voice came from the right. She'd been right behind Camille. The bullet could easily have hit either of them. Jenny lay on the ground, blood gushing from a wound in her shoulder. Camille's stomach flipped as she fell to her knees at her friend's side.

"I don't know what to do." she cried, a lump in her throat.

Jenni grimaced. "Put pressure on the wound."

Camille looked around her frantically. She only had her shirt and jeans. Yanking the shirt over her head, she balled it up and pressed it to the wound. "What now?"

Her blinked slowly as she fought to keep her eyes opened. "Artery. Can't help. Go without me." Her eyes closed and her voice whispered past pale lips. "We can't let them take both of us."

Camille shook her head. "No, I won't just leave you for them to find."

Her friend forced her eyes open and smiled weakly. "They won't take me alive. Find the Ohm. Help fight for other Shines." Jenni's eyes closed and didn't open again.

Tears poured down Camille's face. "No," she whispered struggling to swallow past the lump in her throat. "Please."

She touched her forehead to her best friend's as a sharp pain stabbed into her heart. "Please don't go."

Flashlights swept back and forth across the wheat field, looking for the women. Camille kissed Jenni's forehead. "I love you like a sister."

The flashlights drew closer and Camille could hear voices calling back and forth. She relaxed her hold on her

Shine, so that those approaching would see Jenni. Maybe they'd be able to save her friend. She squeezed Jenni's hand one last time and reluctantly moved away.

As she ran, a shout went up. Silent sobs shook her as she stopped and looked back. Flashlights circled the place where she'd left her friend.

She'd find the Ohm. And after she'd helped save other Shine, she'd make the SSS pay for Jenni's death.

19

Camille hugged Michael. "Thanks for your help."

He shrugged, his face ragged with his grief.

Jenni's body had been found that morning, unrecognizable as it burned inside the black SUV, along with that of Gary and the driver, Crooked Nose. The cops still looked for the woman who'd held a gun on them at the church. Camille was the only one who knew Jeremy had been there. She kept the information to herself, his words making a fool of her. *Look beyond the surface, Camille. Things aren't always what they seem.* She'd keep her promise to Jenni first, but someday she'd hunt Jeremy down and make him pay.

Michael had shown up at the church with Sheriff Saunders, but no sign remained of the SSS. The room where Michael said the cages had been had held couches and a kitchenette that appeared to have been there for years. The walls hadn't even been white, but a dull, faded yellow. The church's main office had been notified of the suspected activities occurring at the Clinton campus. The main office had sworn to do a thorough investigation of Brother Corey and fully cooperate with the police.

No one could prove Jenni had died from anything, but an accident. They'd somehow made the bullet holes vanish. Camille's heart smoldered. The SSS managed to get away with the murders of her parents and her best friend. Grief swelled in her chest, her eyes burned with unshed tears.

"Are you sure you don't want me to come with you?" he asked for the millionth time.

Camille shook her head. "Someone needs to look after

Dr. Pham."

"I can have my father look after him."

"This is my fight, Michael. You have a life here. Family." Camille turned to gaze out into the night. "I don't have anything holding me here. I promised her I'd find the Ohm. That I'd fight. That I'd become that damn lighthouse in the storm she wanted to be. And that's what I'm going to do." She turned back and reached out to squeeze his hand. "I'll contact you when I can to let you know I made it."

Camille walked to Jenni's hatchback, parked in the Phams' driveway, though no one but she and Michael could see it or her. It turned out she could control who or what was affected by her Shine. She climbed into the driver's seat, while Michael rounded her car to his truck also parked in the Phams' driveway.

She rolled down her passenger window. "I'll make them pay for her death, Michael."

He nodded his head and climbed into his truck. She backed Jenni's car out of the drive. After winding through town, she turned onto the highway and pointed the car west toward the California desert. She had a promise to keep.

Acknowledgements

I'd like to thank William Bernhardt for everything he gives back to new writers. He is an amazing teacher and a truly kind person. I'm honored to call him friend. Being asked to contribute to the Shine universe is the biggest compliment on my writing ability that I've ever received and no matter how much I try, I'll never be able to thank him enough.

I'd also like to thank my beautiful hub for believing in me more than I believed in myself. He is my rock and the best typo-catcher ever! I love him more than he'll ever understand.

Thanks to my mom, gram, and siblings for reading and loving my writing. Their support and praise during those first months gave me the confidence to keep going.

About the Author

Sabrina A. Fish is a native Oklahoman. She has a Bachelor's degree in Political Science from the University of Oklahoma. BOOMER SOONER. She attended two of William Bernhardt's small writing seminars. Her writing accolades include first place in the Tragedy Category of the What If? Fairytale Madness Blogfest and placing in Challenge #2 of Rachel Harrie's Platform Building Campaign 4. She also placed in Vine and Leaves Literary Journal's Spring 2013 Vignette Contest. She owns a trophy and awards company with her husband where she collects interesting names for her writing from the lists of winners. She is blessed to be called Mom by what she considers the most beautiful little boy in the universe and enjoys the help of his amazing imagination for some of her story ideas.

Made in the USA
Columbia, SC
04 December 2017